Brutus the Wonder Poodle

By Linda Gondosch

Illustrations by Penny Dann

A STEPPING STONE BOOK

Random House 🏠 New York

To my nephew, Michael Hamers

Library of Congress Cataloging-in-Publication Data
Gondosch, Linda. Brutus, the wonder poodle / by Linda Gondosch ; illustrations by Penny
Dann.   p.   cm.—(A Stepping stone book) Summary: When Ryan's parents give him
a toy poodle puppy, Ryan is disappointed that the dog is not bigger, but quickly learns that
Brutus is the best dog ever. ISBN 0-679-80573-7 (pbk.)—ISBN 0-679-90573-1 (lib. bdg.):
[1. Dogs—Fiction. 2. Toys—Fiction. 3. Size—Fiction.] I. Dann, Penny, ill. II. Title.
PZ7.G587Br 1990 [Fic]—dc20 89-39377

Manufactured in the United States of America   1 2 3 4 5 6 7 8 9 0

Contents

1

The Kids from Clover Lane

On Monday the kids from Clover Lane met on Ryan's front porch. Everyone except Ryan brought a pet. "Let's have the pet show next week," said Cassie, her curly ponytail bobbing up and down as she talked.

Tony stretched out his long legs. "Next month," he said. "Duke hasn't learned how to fetch yet." He patted Duke's head. The boxer wagged his tail, knocking over a flowerpot. Ryan picked it up.

Rosa held a birdcage on her lap. She had brought her parrot. "Aunt Lucy will win the prize for sure," she said. "She can talk. Nobody has a pet that can talk."

"Shut up, stupid. Where's the food? Where's the food?" squawked Aunt Lucy.

"Make your dumb bird be quiet," said Jonathan. He pushed his glasses higher on his nose.

"She's not dumb!" said Rosa. "She's just hungry."

"Shut up, stupid. Where's the food?" said the parrot.

"Hush, Aunt Lucy," scolded Rosa.

"I should win," said Jonathan. "I have the most unusual pet." He held a ferret on the end of a leash. It looked like a skinny rat with a very long neck.

"You have the weirdest pet," said Tony.

"Fred is not weird," said Jonathan.

"He has a long neck, just like you," said Tony.

Jonathan frowned. "I bet your dog can't find mice like Fred can. Fred can find anything. He has a good nose. Don't you, Fred?" Tony's dog sniffed the ferret and backed away.

"Let's have the show tomorrow," said Cassie. She hugged her gray cat. Dusty sat on Cassie's lap and flicked her tail. "Dusty is the prettiest cat in Pigeon Creek. And she can catch a mouse just as fast as Fred."

"She can not," said Jonathan. He pulled Cassie's ponytail.

"Ouch! She can, too," said Cassie. She pulled Jonathan's curly hair.

"I don't want to have a pet show," said Ryan.

"What?" Everyone turned to look at Ryan. He stared down at the floor.

"It's my porch and I don't want a dumb pet show."

"You don't want one because you don't have a pet," said Tony.

"You're right," said Ryan. I want a dog just like Duke, he thought. I would be the happiest boy in Pigeon Creek with a dog like Duke.

"That's okay," said Cassie. "We can still have a pet show. You can be the judge, Ryan. Someone has to be the judge."

"That's no fun," said Ryan. "I want a pet."

"Well, get one," said Jonathan. "How about a snake? I saw one in the woods yesterday. It was a beaut."

"I don't like snakes," said Ryan. He stroked Duke's head. "I want a dog."

"Okay, get a dog," said Jonathan.

"How?" asked Ryan.

"I don't know," answered Jonathan.

"Ask your dad," said Rosa.

"He'll never get me a dog," said Ryan.

"How do you know?" asked Rosa.

"I already asked him—a hundred times," said Ryan.

"How about a flea?" asked Tony. "Duke has lots of fleas."

"All I want is a dog," said Ryan. "Forget the fleas."

2
I Don't Like Lizards

The next day Ryan dropped a pile of library books on the kitchen table. He showed one to his father. It was called *How to Train Your Dog*.

"Isn't this great, Dad?" said Ryan. "I'm going to read all about dogs. And see this notebook? I have a section on dog names. I have another section on how to give a dog a bath. I have another section on—"

"Wait a minute, Ryan," said Mr. Harrison. "We don't have a dog."

"I know that. But I've got a dog leash." Ryan held up a rope. "And see this collar Tony gave me? Duke is too big for it. And look at this terrific dog bed. I got this box from the grocery, and Mom gave me an old towel."

"Is that why you wanted that towel?" asked Mrs. Harrison. "For a doggy blanket?"

"Sure, Mom. I didn't want my dog to catch cold," said Ryan. "Tony gave me some dog food. He gave me a whole bagful. All I need now is a dog."

"Ryan, we don't have room for a dog," said his mother.

"Oh, Mom, a dog doesn't take up any space," said Ryan. "I'll throw away the dog bed. He can sleep with me. I'll be glad to share my bed. Please?"

"Dogs make messes," said Ryan's mother.

"I'll clean them up," said Ryan. "I promise!"

"Dogs need exercise," said Ryan's father.

"I'll take him for a walk every day," said Ryan. "I promise!"

"Dogs shed on the furniture," said Ryan's mother.

"I'll brush him every day. I promise!" said Ryan. "He'll be the cleanest dog in Pigeon Creek."

"We'll have to think about it," said Ryan's father.

"Think fast, okay?" said Ryan. "We're having a pet show. I'm the only one without a pet. Do you know what that feels like?"

"When I was your age," said Ryan's father, "I had a lizard. I got it at the circus. It was long and green and—"

"No lizards!" said Mrs. Harrison. "It might get loose and climb on the sofa. I don't want to sit on a long green lizard."

"Don't worry, Mom," said Ryan. "I don't like lizards. I just want a dog. A dog will protect our house, Mom. A dog will fetch your slippers, Dad. A dog will keep me warm at night. A dog will clean up the floor around the kitchen table. Everybody needs a good dog."

Just then Ryan's four-year-old sister, Molly, walked in. "Me too. I want a dog too!"

"I'm getting a dog, Molly," said Ryan. "Not you."

"No fair," said Molly. "I want one too. You always get everything."

"Who said anyone's getting anything?" said their father.

3
Brutus

By Wednesday, Ryan had almost given up. It didn't look as though his parents had done any more thinking about getting a dog. He was flipping sadly through the dog names in his notebook when he heard the back door open. "Here he is, Ryan," called Mr. Harrison. "Your new pet!"

"What?" Ryan jumped out of his chair. "Really, Dad?" He looked left and right. He looked behind his father. He looked all around the room. His mother and sister joined in the search.

"Where? Where?" Ryan asked. "Where is he?"

"Right here, son." Mr. Harrison patted his jacket pocket. Two little white ears hung over the edge. Two little black eyes stared up at Ryan.

"What is it?" cried Ryan. "A hamster?"

"A toy poodle," said Mr. Harrison. "Your very own puppy." Mr. Harrison put the puppy on the floor. It trembled from head to tail.

"That's no toy," said Ryan. "That's real!"

"A toy poodle is a small poodle," explained Mr. Harrison. "A very small poodle."

"But he's so little," said Ryan. "He doesn't look like Duke at all. Are you sure this is a dog?"

"Of course he's a dog," said his father.

"We can't get a big dog like Duke," said his mother. "Our yard is too small for a big dog."

"He's just right!" cried Molly. "Can I take him for a ride on my tricycle? I'll put him in the basket."

Mr. Harrison ruffled Molly's hair. "This is Ryan's dog, Molly. He's in charge. But don't worry. You'll get to play with him."

"I want to play now!" Molly reached for the puppy, but the puppy ran from the kitchen like a rabbit being chased.

"Uh-oh," said Mrs. Harrison. "Catch him before he soils the carpet."

Ryan and Molly chased the puppy. The faster they ran, the faster the puppy ran. The puppy slid on the kitchen floor and skidded into a cabinet.

"I've got him!" yelled Ryan. But the puppy slipped through his hands and scampered away. Ryan and Molly ran after him. Around

and around they went. Under the dining room table, past the piano, through the hallway, around the TV, over the footstool and then— *plop!* The puppy jumped onto a pillow on the floor. Ryan grabbed him. The puppy yelped and then began to whimper.

"It's all right," said Ryan. He rubbed his cheek against the little dog's curly-haired head. "I won't hurt you." The puppy licked Ryan's cheek.

"I think I'll call him Brutus," he said.

"Brutus?" said Mr. and Mrs. Harrison.

"Brutus. That's a big, tough name. He'll grow into it." Brutus wagged his tiny tail, closed his eyes, and fell asleep.

"I know what we should call him," said Molly. "Fluffy. He looks like a Fluffy."

"Uh-uh," said Ryan. "His name is Brutus."

4

Eat, Brutus, Eat!

On Thursday, Ryan sat in the grass with Brutus. "Listen, Brutus. You've got to be tough. Do you hear? Tough!" Brutus barked. "First of all," said Ryan, "this has got to go." He pulled a pretty blue bow off Brutus's head. "Mom does the dumbest things."

Next Ryan found the old dog collar that Tony had given him. "Here, boy," he called. Brutus ran away from Ryan. "Here, boy, here!" called Ryan. He chased Brutus around the yard. He ran and ran but Brutus ran faster. Finally Ryan fell down into a pile of leaves. Brutus jumped on top of him.

"Gotcha!" said Ryan. He put the leather collar around Brutus's neck. Brutus stepped right out of it.

"Never mind," said Ryan. "You don't need a collar. But you do need to be tough. Do you hear? You need to be big and tough like Duke." Brutus barked.

"What you need is food," said Ryan. "If you want to grow big and strong like Duke, you have to eat." Ryan went into the house.

He came back out with a tray of food. "Now, this is hamburger, Brutus. Eat! And this is cheese and apples and carrots and yogurt. If you want more, here is Duke's dog food. That should do it. You have got to grow, boy. Eat, eat!" So Brutus ate. But he could not finish all of it.

Just then Ryan saw a rabbit hopping across Cassie's yard. "Look!" said Ryan. "Do you see that rabbit, Brutus? Go get him! Get the rabbit! Charge! Go, Brutus, go!" Brutus sniffed the yogurt.

Ryan sighed. "You missed your big chance. The rabbit's gone." Brutus looked up and wagged his tail.

"You're supposed to chase rabbits," said Ryan. "You're supposed to bring them home for dinner. What kind of dog are you, any-way?"

Just then Cassie walked by. "Oh, Ryan! You got a puppy!"

"This is Brutus," said Ryan. Brutus jumped up and down and ran around in circles when he saw Cassie.

"Ooh, isn't he cute!" cried Cassie. "You sweet little itsy-bitsy-witsy cutie pie!"

"What do you want, Cassie?" said Ryan.

"I just want to see your sweet little itsy-bitsy—"

"Brutus is eating dinner now, Cassie."

"Eating? You feed that cute little puppy all that stuff?"

"That's right. Growing puppies need a lot of food."

"Not that stuff! Just a minute."

Cassie ran home. She came back with something in her hand. "Now, this is what I feed my cat. Your sweet little cutie pie will love this."

"What is it?"

"Nibble Wibbles." Cassie held out some Nibble Wibbles. Brutus sniffed them and sneezed.

"My dog does not eat cat food," said Ryan. "Does he look like a cat?"

"Well, yes. He does. Nibble Wibbles are good for him."

"Brutus eats hamburger," said Ryan, "and rabbit. Come on, boy. Let's go hunt rabbits." Brutus lifted his head and listened. Then he bounded away and tumbled headfirst into a pile of leaves.

"Are you sure Brutus isn't a rabbit?" asked Cassie. She laughed.

"Of course he's not a rabbit! He's just small, that's all. But he'll grow."

"My cat is bigger than he is," said Cassie. "When does he start growing, anyway?"

Ryan searched through the leaves trying to find Brutus. "Just you wait, Cassie. Brutus will be as big as Duke. Maybe even bigger. I just have to feed him more hamburger."

5

The Rabbit Chase

On Friday, Ryan continued Brutus's lessons. "Now, this is a rabbit. See?" Ryan held up an old stuffed rabbit. He tied a rope around the stuffed rabbit's leg. Slowly he pulled the rabbit across the yard. Brutus's rear end stuck up in the air. His nose touched the ground. He growled at the stuffed rabbit.

Ryan pulled the rabbit faster and faster. Soon he was running. The rabbit bounced on the ground behind him.

"Get him, Brutus! Get the rabbit. Charge!"

Brutus barked. He dashed for the rabbit and caught it with his tiny teeth.

"Good boy, Brutus! You got the rabbit." Brutus growled. He shook the stuffed rabbit left and right as hard as he could.

"Okay. Let's try it again." Ryan took the rabbit from Brutus, then pulled the rope. Brutus quickly pounced on the toy rabbit.

Suddenly Ryan said, "Shhh! There's a *real* rabbit. Look! He's by the trees." Ryan pointed to a white-tailed rabbit behind a maple tree. The rabbit stood still. Its nose wiggled. "Go get him, Brutus! Get the rabbit. Charge!"

Cassie walked into Ryan's yard. "What are you doing now?" she asked.

"Shhh! Brutus is going to catch that rabbit."

"What rabbit?"

"Over there." Ryan pointed to the rabbit by the tree.

"I can't see it," said Cassie.

Brutus stood up tall. He looked all around. Suddenly he spotted the rabbit. He barked and the rabbit hopped away.

"Go get him, Brutus! Get the rabbit."

"What do you want an old rabbit for?" asked Cassie. "Why don't you teach him to chase mice? They're more his size." She laughed. "Come here, you sweet little itsy-bitsy puppy dog." Brutus wiggled up to Cassie and wagged his whole body.

"Look what I brought you today," said Cassie. "Nibble Wibbles!" Brutus licked his lips and jumped.

"Let me see you dance." Cassie held up a Nibble Wibble. "Dance, dance!" Brutus stood on his back legs and took a step or two. "That's good. Now turn around."

"Stop it, Cassie," said Ryan.

"Poodles are good dancers," said Cassie. "Come on, Foo-Foo. Dance!"

"His name is not Foo-Foo. And he can't dance."

But Brutus could dance. He danced back and forth and left and right and ate the Nibble Wibbles.

"Come, Brutus!" ordered Ryan. He grabbed the rope and pulled the stuffed rabbit. "Get the rabbit!" But Brutus just sat in the grass. He was busy crunching and munching a Nibble Wibble.

6

Go Get Him, Brutus!

Saturday was cold and windy. Brutus whined at the door. "Quick!" called Mrs. Harrison. "Brutus needs to go outside."

"It's cold outside," said Molly.

"Look what I have," said Mrs. Harrison. She opened a bag. Out came a new sweater for Brutus. It was soft and yellow with pink and blue flowers all over it. Mrs. Harrison slipped it over Brutus's head. She folded down the turtleneck collar.

"Now, isn't that the cutest thing you ever saw?" she asked.

"Aw, Mom," said Ryan. "Brutus can't wear a silly thing like that."

"Why not?"

Mom just doesn't understand, thought Ryan. He ran to his closet and found his old brown leather jacket. It was much too small for him. He cut off a sleeve and cut two holes in it for Brutus's front legs. He ran back to the kitchen. "Where's Brutus?"

"Uh-oh," said Mr. Harrison. "Too late." Brutus stood by the door. A puddle was next to him.

"Puppy puddle!" said Molly.

Ryan cleaned up the puddle. Then he took off Brutus's sweater. "Now, here is a coat to be proud of." He pushed the brown leather coat over Brutus's head. It did not fit as well as the yellow sweater, but Brutus did not mind.

"I'm taking Brutus for a walk," said Ryan.

"In that thing?" asked Mrs. Harrison. "It looks like a bag."

"It's a good, warm coat," said Ryan. "Brutus will grow into it."

"I want to go too," said Molly.

"No," said Ryan.

"Yes!" said Molly.

Ryan and Molly and Brutus walked down the sidewalk. Brutus's white ears flopped up and down. He bounced along happily with his tail held high.

Tony and Jonathan were tossing a football in Jonathan's yard. "What's that?" asked Tony. He stared at Brutus.

"Dad got me a dog! His name is Brutus," said Ryan.

"That's a dog?" said Tony. "He sure is small."

"Hey, Brutus. Fetch!" yelled Jonathan. He threw the football. Brutus wagged his tail.

"He looks mean," said Tony. He reached over and patted the puppy. Brutus rolled onto his back and waved his paws in the air.

"Yeah. Real dangerous," said Jonathan.

"He *is* dangerous," said Ryan. "He bites . . . sometimes."

Duke suddenly trotted into the yard. His ears stood straight up. He had his eye on Brutus.

Molly cried, "Look out, Brutus! Duke will kill you!"

"Be quiet, Molly!" said Ryan. "Brutus can take care of himself."

Brutus saw Duke and rolled over. Then he crouched, his rear end high in the air. His nose touched the ground. All at once he leaped forward with a bark and charged at Duke.

"Attaboy, Brutus! Go get him, Brutus!" called Ryan. Molly covered her eyes.

Brutus stopped in front of Duke's nose and stood very still. Duke's tail began to move

slowly back and forth. He inched toward the
little dog. Brutus turned and ran around the
yard. Duke chased him. The closer Duke got
to Brutus, the faster Brutus ran.

"Wait, Brutus!" yelled Ryan. "Don't run away!" But Brutus slipped between the fence posts and ran down the sidewalk. Duke stopped when he reached the fence. He jumped at the fence and barked.

"That's the smallest dog I ever saw," said Tony.

"Brutus might be small, but he's dangerous," said Ryan. "He probably didn't want to hurt Duke. Brutus can really bite. His teeth are like needles."

"He's cute," said Jonathan.

"Great! Now we can have our pet show," said Tony. "I'll go tell everyone."

Ryan didn't say anything, but he still wasn't too happy about the pet show. Brutus wasn't ready. Ryan wondered if he would ever be ready.

7

Puppy School

On Sunday, Ryan couldn't face teaching Brutus anymore. But Cassie came over with a rubber bone. "I bought this for my cat," she said. "But Dusty doesn't like rubber bones. Here, Brutus. Fetch!" She tossed the bone across the yard.

Brutus ran and searched for the bone. He sniffed the ground. There it was! He bit into the bone and began to chew. "Bring it here!" called Cassie. "Bring it here!"

Brutus looked up. He stopped chewing. He held his head to one side and looked at Cassie. Cassie stomped her foot. She pointed to the ground. "I said to bring it here," she called. "Hurry up!"

Brutus trotted over to Cassie. He wagged his tail. Cassie took the rubber bone from his mouth. "Good boy, Brutus. Good dog." She patted his head.

"What are you doing, Cassie?" asked Ryan.

"I'm teaching Brutus to fetch. Poodles are good at running and fetching. Watch this." Cassie took off her sneaker. She threw it across the yard. It landed near a bush. "Fetch, Brutus. Go fetch!"

Brutus barked and ran to the bush. He sniffed all around the bush until he found the sneaker. He sat down and began to chew it.

"Bring it here!" yelled Cassie. "Come on, Brutus. Bring it here!" But Brutus wouldn't come.

Ryan laughed. "Good luck getting your shoe back."

"I'll give you a Nibble Wibble," Cassie called.

Brutus jumped up with the sneaker in his mouth and ran to Cassie. He dropped the sneaker in front of her. Cassie gave him a Nibble Wibble.

"Dogs will do anything for Nibble Wibbles," said Cassie. She put her shoe back on.

"Hey, that's not bad," said Ryan.

"I wish Dusty could run and fetch," said Cassie.

"Look, Brutus." Ryan pulled a paper-wrapped candy kiss from his pocket. He let Brutus sniff it. "That's candy, Brutus. Fetch!" He tossed the candy kiss across the yard. Brutus jumped up and found the candy kiss.

"Okay, bring it here!" ordered Ryan.

But Brutus decided to eat the candy. "No, no, Brutus," said Cassie. "Candy is bad for your teeth." She pulled the candy kiss from Brutus's mouth. "Here, you sweet little puppy, have another Nibble Wibble." Brutus barked and stood on his back legs.

"Look!" cried Cassie. "He's dancing for me!"

"Yeah," said Ryan. "But I still wish he could hunt rabbits."

"Brutus can run and fetch and dance," said Cassie. "And you know what? I bet we could teach him to jump through a hoop and roll over, too."

"You think so?" asked Ryan.

"Brutus is smart," said Cassie. "I wish Dusty could jump through a hoop."

"Brutus *is* smart," agreed Ryan. "Watch this." Ryan sat down on the ground. "Give me a kiss, Brutus," he said. Brutus jumped up and licked Ryan's face. His tail wagged as fast as it could.

Ryan sprawled out in the grass. He laughed and hugged his puppy. "That's his best trick."

8

Who Gets First Prize?

A week later Ryan and his friends held their pet show. Other Clover Lane kids gathered in Ryan's front yard. They sat in rows of chairs and waited. The pet show was about to begin.

"I want to hold Brutus," said Molly.

"Not now, Molly," said Ryan. "You're not in this show."

"I'm telling. You won't let me do anything." Molly stomped away.

Cassie came running with her cat under one arm. Under her other arm was a purple purse. "I got the prizes," she called.

"It's about time," said Jonathan.

"I had to buy them," said Cassie. "I got them with the money we chipped in." She opened the purse and pulled out a peppermint stick. "Third prize is a peppermint stick." She pulled out a jumbo chocolate bar. "Second prize is a candy bar."

"What's first prize?" asked Jonathan. He was sure his ferret would win first prize.

"Three dollars and sixteen cents," said Cassie. "That's all the money that was left."

"I could use three dollars and sixteen cents," said Jonathan. "Who's the judge?"

"They are," said Rosa. She pointed to the boys and girls sitting on the chairs. Molly came back. She sat in the front row. Her lower lip stuck out. Her arms were crossed on her chest.

"When does the show start?" asked Nathan Hall. He set his little sister Sarah on the chair next to him. "I have to go to the dentist at two o'clock."

"The show is starting now," said Jonathan. He held up his ferret for everyone to see. "This is Fred. He's a member of the weasel family. He's also the best mouse hunter in the world. He can go through holes, crawl under logs, and squeeze through a tear in a screen door. One time he got into our kitchen cabinet. You should have heard my mom yell."

"Let's see him catch a mouse," said a girl with pigtails.

"Okay," said Jonathan. He put Fred on the ground. Fred ran across the front yard to the garage, crawled under Molly's tricycle, and hid behind the garbage can.

While Jonathan went to look for him the show went on. "Let me show you my beautiful cat," said Cassie. She put her purple purse down on a table. Then she picked up Dusty for everyone to see. "My cat gives herself a bath every morning. When she had kittens, she gave all of them baths. She's a very clean cat. She likes to play with yarn." Cassie dangled a piece of yarn in front of her cat. Dusty rubbed against Cassie's leg and purred. Then she purred some more.

"She's not playing with the yarn," said Molly.

"Well, she did yesterday," said Cassie.

"I want to see some tricks," called Nathan Hall.

"You want to see tricks?" said Tony. "I'll show you tricks. My dog, Duke, can do tricks. Watch this!" Tony threw a large yellow ball into the air. Duke leaped up with a sharp bark. He chased the ball down the driveway.

Chomp. Duke grabbed the ball with his teeth.

"Here, Duke. Here boy! Bring me the ball," called Tony. Everyone watched Duke. But Duke had other plans. He turned and trotted down the street. "Come back here!" ordered Tony. He ran down the driveway. "Get over here, Duke! Bad dog!" Tony chased his dog down the street.

"It's my turn," said Rosa. She held up her

birdcage. "This is Aunt Lucy. Say hello, Aunt Lucy. Say hello."

Aunt Lucy blinked her orange eyes. "Awk!" she squawked.

"Parrots cost a lot of money," said Rosa. "My grandmother gave Aunt Lucy to us when she moved back to Mexico. Parrots are very smart birds. They can talk and sing songs and recite poetry. *Mary Had a Little Lamb.* Come on, Aunt Lucy. Say *Mary Had a Little Lamb.*"

"I think Aunt Lucy is sleeping," said Molly.

"Shut up, stupid. Where's the food? Where's the food?" squawked Aunt Lucy.

Everybody laughed. "Aunt Lucy gets first prize!" the boys and girls yelled. "Give her a cracker." They clapped their hands.

"Wait a minute," said Ryan. "You haven't seen Brutus yet."

9
Tricks and Stolen Treats

"We like Aunt Lucy. We like Aunt Lucy," chanted all the boys and girls except Molly. Nathan's sister danced around the yard.

"Sit down! Sit down, everyone," ordered Cassie. "You have to see Ryan's pet, too."

Tony walked back into the front yard. He tried to pull Duke along. But Duke was hard to pull. Duke wanted to go home. "Sit, Duke, sit!" ordered Tony. Duke would not sit. He stood with his feet spread apart.

"This is my dog, Brutus," said Ryan. "He's a toy poodle."

"That's a toy?" asked the girl with the pigtails. "He looks real to me."

"He is real," said Ryan. "A toy poodle is a very small poodle." He held Brutus up. Brutus wagged his tail and almost wiggled out of Ryan's hands.

"Aw, isn't that a cute little puppy," said Nathan.

"He's my puppy too," said Molly. She reached for Brutus.

"Wait, Molly. Let me finish," said Ryan. "Brutus is small but he's smart," he continued. "He knows all kinds of tricks."

"Show them how he dances," called Cassie. She pulled some Nibble Wibbles from her pocket. "Here, Ryan. You might need these."

"Thanks," said Ryan. He set Brutus down on the ground and waved his hand in a circle. "Okay, Brutus. Roll over! Roll over!" Brutus stretched out on the ground like a rug and then rolled onto his back. His paws pointed straight up.

"Roll over!" ordered Ryan. "All the way over." Brutus rolled all the way over. Then he jumped to his feet with a bark. Everyone laughed.

"I like Brutus!" said Sarah Hall.

"He's my puppy too," said Molly. She reached for Brutus.

"Wait, Molly. I'm not done," said Ryan.

"Awk! Shut up, stupid. Where's the food?" said the parrot.

Ryan gave Brutus a Nibble Wibble. "Would Aunt Lucy like a Nibble Wibble?" Ryan asked Rosa. He handed a Nibble Wibble to Rosa.

"Okay, Brutus, let's jump!" called Ryan. He held out a stick. "Jump!" Brutus looked at Ryan and wagged his tail. Then he ran and jumped over the stick.

"Attaboy!" said Ryan. He gave Brutus another Nibble Wibble.

"Hooray for Brutus!" shouted all the boys and girls.

"Let's show everyone how you can fetch, okay?" asked Ryan. Brutus barked. The little dog was enjoying himself. He liked to play. Doing tricks was just like playing. He also liked Nibble Wibbles.

Ryan threw his old stuffed rabbit as far as he could. "Go fetch, Brutus! Go fetch!" Brutus bounded after the rabbit. He picked it up and shook it left and right. "Here, Brutus! Bring it here!" ordered Ryan. Brutus perked up his ears. He wanted to play with the rabbit. He shook it hard. "Here, Brutus! Bring it here!" shouted Ryan. Everyone watched Brutus. Brutus carried the rabbit back to Ryan. He wagged his tail when Ryan gave him another Nibble Wibble.

Everyone clapped their hands and stamped their feet. "We want Brutus! We want Brutus!" they chanted.

"He's my puppy too," said Molly.

"Show them how Brutus can dance," said Cassie.

"No, no. That's enough," said Ryan, embarrassed.

"I want to see Brutus dance," yelled Nathan.

"Me too," said his sister.

Ryan looked at Tony. Tony held Duke's chain and shouted with the rest, "We want to see Brutus dance!"

Ryan looked at Jonathan. Jonathan was busy clapping his hands and watching Brutus. "Dance, Brutus, dance!" he called.

Ryan decided to show everyone just what a talented dog he had. "Okay, Brutus, dance!" He twirled his hand in the air and Brutus danced. Just like a circus dog, he hopped about on his back legs. He turned in circles. He waved his front paws. His white ears flopped up and down.

"Hooray for Brutus!" called all the boys and girls. "Brutus wins the prize."

Cassie stood up. She looked for her purple purse. It wasn't on the table. "My purse!" she cried. "It's gone!"

"What?" said Jonathan. "Gone?"

"There were three dollars and sixteen cents, a peppermint stick, and a jumbo chocolate bar in that purse," said Cassie. "I put it on this table. I know I did."

"Who took it?" asked Tony.

"Not me," said Molly.

"Not me," said Nathan.

"I sure didn't," said Jonathan.

"Well, who did?" asked Cassie.

10
Catch That Thief!

"There's the thief!" yelled Rosa. She pointed across the front lawn. Fred the ferret was running down the driveway. His skinny body slunk along the ground. Cassie's purse was clutched in his mouth.

"Get him!" called Jonathan. "He'll get away. I'll never find him."

Everyone jumped up and ran after Fred. "He'll eat the candy!" cried Cassie. "He'll eat my purse!"

They left Aunt Lucy behind. "Awk!" she squawked. "Awk! Where's the food?" But nobody heard her.

Duke galloped after the ferret but stopped suddenly. He sat and scratched at some fleas. He scratched and scratched. When fleas bit Duke, he always took time to scratch.

Dusty followed behind Cassie for a little way. Then the cat turned left and walked back to her own porch. She sprang onto a sunny railing. "Come on, Dusty!" called Cassie. But Dusty decided to take a nap instead.

Jonathan's ferret zigzagged through three yards. Then he headed for the woods and disappeared into a clump of trees.

"We'll never find him!" said Jonathan. "I never should have taken off his leash."

"Go get him, Brutus. Go fetch! Go fetch the rabbit," ordered Ryan.

"Fred's not a rabbit," said Jonathan. "He's a ferret."

Brutus dashed into the woods. He sniffed the ground. Then he hopped over a rock. He climbed through a hollow log. He slid under a fallen tree trunk. He scampered around a bush. He sniffed some more.

"Where's Fred, Brutus? Go fetch! Go fetch the rabbit," ordered Ryan.

"Fred's not a rabbit," said Jonathan.

"Fred's a thief!" said Rosa. "But Brutus will catch him. Won't he, Ryan?"

"I hope so," said Ryan. He ran faster.

"Hey, Duke!" yelled Tony. "Come, Duke!" Duke was busy scratching and didn't even look up.

Brutus ran deeper into the woods. He held his nose to the ground. Then he sniffed the air. Suddenly he turned right and ran around a tree. There was Fred, digging at a hole in the tree trunk. The purple purse lay on the ground. Brutus barked at Fred. Then he grabbed the purse between his teeth. He dragged it away from the tree. He sat down and began to chew the purse.

"Brutus!" called Ryan. Everyone gathered around.

"Fred!" called Jonathan. "You're in big trouble, Fred."

"Here, Brutus. Bring it here, boy," ordered

Ryan. Brutus shook the purse as hard as he could.

"Brutus! Bring it here! Bring me the purse!" Brutus stopped shaking the purse. He tilted his head to one side. Then he jumped up and ran to Ryan.

"Good boy! Good Brutus," Ryan said. He lifted Brutus up in his arms. "You're such a good dog."

"Brutus gets first prize," said Nathan.

"First prize for Brutus!" cried all the children.

"That's some dog you've got there, Ryan," said Jonathan. He carried his ferret on his shoulder.

"I know," said Ryan proudly.

"He's the smallest dog I ever saw," said Tony. "But he sure is smart."

"He's my puppy too," said Molly.

"Do you think I could teach Duke how to run and fetch?" asked Tony.

"You have to feed him Nibble Wibbles," said Cassie. "Dogs will do anything for a treat."

"That's what I'll buy with the prize money," said Ryan. "A box of Nibble Wibbles. We'll give Duke some lessons."

"I wish I had a dog like Brutus," said Jonathan.

A vote was taken. Rosa won the jumbo candy bar for having a bird that could talk. Cassie won the peppermint stick for having the cleanest and prettiest pet. She broke off a piece and gave it to Tony. "For the biggest dog," she said. She gave Jonathan some, too.

Ryan knew he would never have the biggest dog. But he had a dog that could do tricks. He had a dog that could catch ferrets. Ryan was sure he had the best dog in the whole world.

"Want to see Brutus's best trick?" Ryan asked. He plopped down on the ground. "Give me a kiss, Brutus," he said. Brutus jumped on Ryan. His tail wagged as fast as it could. He licked Ryan's face.

"Me too!" said Molly. She sat on the ground next to Ryan. "Gimme a kiss, too." Brutus jumped up and gave Molly a puppy kiss, too.

About the Author

"When my son, Stephen, was younger, he used to play with his friend's golden retriever," says LINDA GONDOSCH. "Stephen begged for a dog of his own, so we brought home a very small poodle that looked like a snowball. The story of Brutus the Wonder Poodle was born as I watched my son romping with his new pint-size dog. Love between friends has nothing to do with size."

Linda Gondosch lives with her husband and four children, a toy poodle, and sixteen tropical fish in Lawrenceburg, Indiana, on the banks of the Ohio River.

About the Illustrator

PENNY DANN has illustrated many books of poetry and fiction, as well as children's books. She often travels to Paris, where she goes "poodle-spotting," an activity that was helpful to her when she worked on *Brutus the Wonder Poodle.* She lives in Brighton, England.